Slickfester Dude
Tells Bedtime Stories

Life Lessons from our Animal Friends

BY CAROL DUERKSEN (AND SLICKFESTER DUDE)
ILLUSTRATED BY SUSAN BARTEL

Carol

WILLOWSPRING DOWNS

Slickfester Dude

Table of Contents

A Note From Slickfester Dude

These stories are true. The names in this book have not been changed, and the animals are real. We all live together on a Kansas farm called Willowspring Downs with our people Carol and Maynard. (Well, a few of our neighbors make it into the book too.) These stories all happened pretty much the way I tell them, though the words the people and animals say to each other may not be the exact words they said at the time. But they're close enough to give you the idea. And yes, I really did sit on Carol's chest in bed and ask her to hold my hand — excuse me — paw.

Once you read my stories, I think you'll agree — Willowspring Downs is a fascinating place to live. And, as you'll see, often as not, there's more to the goings on than first meets the eye.

Come, listen to our bedtime stories.

Where Reuben Goes

The night the stories started, I was lying in bed with my husband Maynard, not far from sleep. I felt the waterbed move softly, and Slickfester Dude, our black cat, three-legged his way across the covers toward me. Slick's right front leg had been permanently folded across his chest since before we found him, so everything he did was in a three-legged mode.

"Hey, Slick, how're you doin', Dude?" I greeted him.

Slick responded by sitting down squarely on my chest. Gazing at me with those big gold eyes, he reached out his good front paw toward me.

"What?" I asked.

"I want to hold hands," Slick said.

"You want to hold hands."

"Yes. I'd like to hold hands. It makes me feel secure."

"Okay." I took his paw with my fingers and held it.

"Thank you. That feels good." Slick was quiet for awhile, then he said. "Would you like to know a secret?"

"Sure! Tell me a secret."

"I know where Reuben goes."

"You do? Where?"

Now I must explain here about Reuben. Reuben is a black pug dog. For the last few days, Reuben hadn't been around the house at all during the day, and when he showed up in the evening to eat, he looked and smelled bad. Actually, he'd been looking and smelling more like a pig than a pug.

Slick just looked at me, so I asked again. "So where does Reuben go?"

"Down by the creek, where that crippled pig is living in the mud. He sits there with that pig."

"You've gotta be kidding."

"I told you it was a secret. I didn't say it was a lie."

"Sorry. I believe you. But why? Why would Reuben spend days with a sick pig? Especially when his best friend is a chocolate labrador. Who would leave a dog for a hog?"

"Maybe because the pig needs him." Slick looked especially wise when he said that.

Now it was my turn to think for awhile. Yes, that porker had been the victim of domestic violence in the pig pen. Maynard had moved him outside the pen, away from his abusers. Somehow, the hog found his way down to the creek, where the shade trees and mud soothed his wounds. But what could Reuben do for him?

"But how?" I asked Slick. "How does the pig need Reuben?"

"He just needs him to be there. To sit beside him."

"Oh," I said. "You really think that makes a difference?"

"We'll see," Slick said, taking his paw back from me. He began to lick it, and then to give himself a face wash.

"Well thanks for telling me where Reuben's been," I said. "I'm going to sleep now. Goodnight, Slick."

"Goodnight, Carol."

A Pug and a Pig

"I've been watching Reuben and the pig," Slick announced to me several nights later. This time I'd barely made it under the covers before he made his way across the bed, sat down, and gave me his paw.

"Oh?"

"The pig's up and walking around. He seems to think he'll live after all."

"Was there ever any doubt?"

"Oh, you know how it is. Sometimes a pig — or a cat, or a person — wonders if you're gonna get through it all."

"True. Those times do hit us all."

"It's a good thing the pig had Reuben."

"You really think he made a difference?"

"Look, Carol," Slick said almost impatiently. "That pug has been sitting with that pig day and night for days. You can't tell me that kind of dedication doesn't make a difference in the pig's outlook on life."

"You're probably right."

"Of course I'm right."

"What does Rupp the labrador think about this? About his friend Reuben spending so much time in the mud with a pig?" I asked.

"He thinks it's stupid," Slick yawned. "Rupp is handsome. Good-looking. One of the beautiful dogs of the world. He totally doesn't understand why Reuben would leave him — even temporarily — to be nice to an ugly hog."

"It doesn't make sense, does it?"

"Yes, it makes sense," Slick countered. "Doing what's right always makes sense. It just isn't always the easy or fun thing to do."

"You're right, Slickfester Dude," I said.

Slick gazed at me awhile.

"Carol, if something happened to me and I needed you to sit

beside me, would you?"

"Of course I would."

"Good. Goodnight, Carol."

"Goodnight, Slickfester Dude."

Just Jump

One night I could tell Slick had a great story to tell. He practically ran across the bed to plop himself in front of my face.

"Yes?" I said. "You have a good bedtime story for me tonight?"

"The best," Slick said.

"Well?"

Slick started taking his evening bath. There he sat, cleaning himself, not even noticing my impatience. "Hello!" I said. "A story?"

"I was walking in the fields and pastures today. I'm dirty," he said, not even looking at me.

"That's a lot of walking for you to be doing."

Then he did look at me, and his eyes registered just a little bit of disgust. "Being three-legged doesn't mean I can't do things. Like I said, I was out walking."

"Okay, okay. What did you see?"

"I saw the sheep grazing in the wheat field. The field

on top of the hill. The one with the electric fence around it to keep them in."

"Yeah, I know where you mean. Were the sheep okay?"

"All except two. They were out. They were happily eating grass on the wrong side of the fence. They weren't even close to the rest of the herd."

"Stupid sheep."

"Your friend Charity was out there, doing her daily walk. She saw those sheep that were out, and went over there to put them in. I watched from the grass nearby. She lowered the electric fence so it was grounded, and she told the sheep they should jump across and go find the rest of their family. I heard her say it."

"Did they listen?"

"Are you kidding? They looked at her like 'Yeah, right, lady, we know what happens with those wires. We get zapped. No way. Besides, we're quite happy here. The grass is greener.'"

"And then what did Charity do?"

"She told them that it was safe and they could just jump over. 'Besides,' she told them, 'it might seem safe and wonderful now, but after dark it gets dangerous. You won't want to be on the wrong side of the fence. You'll want to be with the rest of the herd, where Reebok the llama can protect you from wild animals.' She told them that, but they just stared at her for awhile and then went back to eating."

Slick picked up where he'd left off with his bath. I waited.

"I guess she finally decided to force them over if she could," Slick eventually continued. "She got behind each of them and clapped her hands and shouted 'JUMP!' One of them did it just right. But the other one hit the wire with his foot. He looked at her all mad-like with his big sheep-eyes and I knew what he was thinking. He had trusted her but he had gotten hurt and he was still on the wrong side."

"Poor Charity. What a mess."

"Well she wasn't giving up. She looked right back at him and said 'I told you to JUMP!' Then she yelled it again and clapped her hands and slapped him on the rump. That time he got over."

"Wow! That's a good story."

"I'm not done yet."

"Oh, sorry."

"When Charity bent down to put the fence back up, I came walking out of the grass. She was surprised to see me, and she offered to carry me back to the farm. That was fine with me. I never turn down rides with friends."

"Only from strangers."

"Huh?"

"You wouldn't take a ride from a stranger."

"Oh, right. Never. Anyway, we followed those two wayward sheep until we saw the rest of the herd. They took off running to join them, and everybody was happy again."

"That's a great story, Slick."

"I'm not done yet!"

"My mistake. I thought when everybody lived happily ever after, the story was over."

"Well there's more to this one. Charity told me as we walked back to the farm that in the Bible, people are often compared to sheep, and Jesus is the Good Shepherd. She said that she thinks sometimes God has to shout at us and push us to get over electric fences in our lives. We sometimes need that kind of encouragement to trust God. God knows what's on the other side, and the good things God has for us far outweigh the risk of getting zapped. We just have to learn to trust."

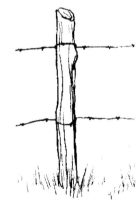

Slick gave his paw one final lick.

"And that's the end of the story," he said.

"You're right, it's the best yet. Goodnight, Slick."

"Goodnight, Carol."

(*Just Jump* by Charity Bucher, Hillsboro, KS.)

Everybody Needs A Friendly Sock

"She's doing it again," Slick announced one evening as he loped across the bed covers and settled in front of my face. Downstairs, I could hear Tjej making loud cat noises.

(Tjej is a Swedish word for "girl" and it's pronounced "Shay." So don't get all worked up saying "tuh-jeege" or something like that. Just say "Shay." And she's Siamese.)

"Sounds like she's got her sock," I said to Slick, who rolled his eyes.

"She is so strange," he said.

Moments later Tjej showed up in the bedroom. In her mouth was a rolled up pair of socks. She set them down, said a few words, and lay down beside them.

"When did this all start?" Slick wanted to know.

"When she was a young girl. She played with socks she found in the clean laundry basket," I explained. "She carried them around like a doll and talked to them."

"But she's not a girl anymore. So what's her problem?"

"Actually, she quit for awhile. Until she had kids of her own. Then she started again, as if to teach them about playing sock."

"I saw one in the food dish one day," Slick said. "And another time, it was in the water pan."

"I know. She treats them as if they're alive. Like they're friends."

"I saw one on the bed next to her grown-up son Lloyd. Does that mean he's doing it too?" Slick sounded quite disgusted.

"I don't think so. I saw Tjej put that sock there, next to him, while he was taking a nap," I said. "In fact, she did that to me once."

"She gave you the sock?"

"Yep, I was taking a nap and when I woke up, the sock was laying against my arm. As if Tjej was giving it to me to be my friend."

"Very peculiar," Slick said. "It's probably because she's Siamese."

"What do you mean by that?"

"Weird cats, those Siamese."

"Any weirder than black cats?"

"What do you mean by that?" Sickfester Dude sat up straight and glared at me.

"I mean all of you cats are unique and special because of what's inside of you, and your color or breeding isn't what's important."

"Well it's what's inside of that Siamese that's strange."

"Slickfester Dude! I disagree! We could use more sock givers in this world!"

Slick didn't look at me. In fact, his eyes closed, and I thought he might have gone to sleep. But he must have been thinking, because when he did open his eyes, he slowly got up from the bed and dropped to the floor. He sidled up to Tjej and did something I'd never seen him do before. He gave Tjej a brief lick on the face. She stared at him with her big blue Siamese eyes, and then she meowed once. It sounded a lot like "Thanks, Dude."

"Goodnight, Tjej," I called from the bed. "Goodnight, Slick."

Pepsi and Paytuh

"Tjej got a letter from her daughter Fresca," Slick announced one evening from his usual position in front of my face. "You know, the kitten you gave to the Goossens."

"Yes, I remember. The beautiful frosty-white one with the soft gray ears."

"Fresca said they have an unusual deal on their yard with Grandma Goossen, a dog named Pepsi, and a goose named Paytuh."

"Paytuh? What kind of name is Paytuh?"

"It's German for Peter. That's what Fresca told Tjej anyway."

"That makes sense. Grandma Goossen is over 90 years old, and Low German is still her first language."

"Anyway, it seems that this Paytuh

goose was a hand-me-down. He came to the family over fourteen years ago, and he'd lived with two other families before that."

"That's a very old goose."

"An old goose with quite a story. When they first got him, he had several wives. But after he lost both of them to coyotes, he just attached himself to Grandma."

"Meaning. . .?"

"He sleeps outside her door. He honks at her from outside. And he protects her from anyone or anything that comes to the house. Including her own son. He grabs at Grandma's son Arlo and pinches him hard. One time the goose got Arlo when they were picking cherries by the creek. Arlo grabbed Paytuh and threw him in the creek. But Paytuh came back and bit Arlo in the rear."

Slick laughed. So did I, and the waterbed shook.

"But there's somebody who can control Paytuh — Pepsi, the dog."

"What kind of dog is Pepsi?"

"He's big and black — part Doberman, part Great Dane."

"My guess is a dog like that could do more than control a goose. He could take care of him permanently."

"No doubt. But not Pepsi. Because you see, Pepsi and Paytuh are best friends. They hang out together. They take naps together on an old cushion in the yard. And if the goose wakes up and the dog doesn't get up when the goose is ready to go for a walk, he picks on the dog, biting him and making that loud honking goose-noise."

"He's asking for trouble."

"You know it. In fact, sometimes Pepsi takes Paytuh's head in his mouth and walks off, dragging that goose with his wings flapping like crazy."

"And he doesn't hurt him?"

"The family says they've thought

more than once that had to be the end of Paytuh. But not at all. Once Pepsi has given Paytuh his lesson, he lets him go.

"And they're jealous of each other when it comes to being close to Grandma. The goose likes to go to the patio window and visit Grandma. She talks to him, and he talks back. Sometimes, when people are trying to talk to each other in the yard, he wants in on the conversation and he's so noisy no one else can talk."

"What does Fresca think of Paytuh?"

"She doesn't like him. He picks on her and the other cats."

"So he doesn't spend all his time with Pepsi?"

"Oh, no. He even helps babysit the baby ducks."

"No!"

"That's what Fresca told Tjej. He runs the mother duck off the nest and he babysits until about 5:00. Then he gets up and walks off. He's done."

"You're not making this up?"

"I am not making this up."

"Sounds like a very interesting farmyard and family."

"You know what Fresca said? She said that Goossen family knows what it means to belong to each other and take care of each other. They're always doing things together. She said maybe Pepsi and Paytuh learned from the people." Slick paused and looked at me. "Do you think that's possible?"

"Yes I do, Slickfester Dude. Don't you?"

"Are we learning from each other?" Slick asked.

"I think so, Slick, when we take the time to pay attention."

"I'm glad we take this time before we go to sleep."

"So am I. Goodnight, Slick."

"Goodnight, my friend."

Sammy's Miracle

Sometimes, a person wants to keep things equal, you know? So I was really happy when something happened that I could tell Slick about during our bedtime conversations. That way, it didn't seem like he was doing all the talking and I was doing all the listening. One of those times was a Sunday evening.

"A very interesting thing happened in Sunday school today," I told Slick as he settled down and looked at me with his big yellow eyes. "But the story begins a long time ago — well, a few years anyway."

"I'm listening," Slick said.

"Well, a few years ago, a stray dog showed up on our farm. Do you remember? It was a yellow retriever type of dog — very sweet and friendly."

"Yes, I think I remember. Didn't. . ."

"Don't spoil the story, Slick, even if you

remember some of it. I want to tell the whole thing."

"Okay, okay, go ahead."

"Like I was saying, this dog showed up. We couldn't keep her — we had too many dogs already."

"You can say that again."

"Yes, we had too many dogs. Well, this one didn't have a tag, so we didn't know where she came from. I was going to run an ad in the paper, but the evening before I did that, I went to the high school Christmas concert. I sat next to a friend of mine named Dorothy who lives on a small farm, and I asked her if she didn't need a dog, because we had a stray show up at our place."

"I love this story."

"Dorothy said she just might be in the market for a dog," I said, ignoring Slick's comment. "She said their dog disappeared, and they might want another one."

"Yes!"

"I began to describe the stray to her, and she said 'That sounds a lot like Sammy! Our dog that disappeared!"

"Do tell!"

"Well the family came over, and sure enough, we had their Sammy! We have no idea why she came to our place — we live five miles apart — but we sure were all happy that she did, and that I asked Dorothy at the concert if she needed a dog.

"What a stroke of luck."

"Maybe."

"What do you mean, maybe?"

"Maynard and I teach junior high boys Sunday school. One of the boys in the class is Winston, Dorothy's son. Our lesson today was on miracles. At the end, we went around the table and asked the guys if they could think of any miracles that had ever happened in their lives. They were all quiet — I guess because they couldn't imagine God doing miracles in their lives today. And then Winston raised his hand and said, 'The day Sammy came home!'"

Slick didn't say anything — he just looked at me. Finally he asked, "So you think it was a miracle and not a stroke of luck?"

"I think it was a stroke of God. On the canvas of our lives, I believe Sammy's return was a brush stroke from God."

"My, my, my, you're getting fancy with your words now. Are you trying to do stories better than me?" Slick smiled. "Anyway, I believe what you're saying, and it's a wonderful story."

"Thank you," I said sleepily.

"Goodnight," said Slickfester Dude.

The Bad Shepherd

Christmas Day evening. Slick hadn't come to bed yet, and I was secretly hoping he wouldn't. I didn't call him. I hoped he'd fallen asleep someplace else. I didn't want to talk tonight.

"Hey!" Slick showed up, meowing his way across the floor and up onto the bed. "I fell asleep on the blanket under the Christmas tree. Sorry about that!"

"No problem," I muttered, and I knew I didn't sound like myself at all.

Slick looked at me.

"Sounds like there's a problem," he said, settling in front of me. "What is it?"

I turned my face away from Slick's, and swallowed hard several times. But it didn't work, and pretty soon there were tears.

"Tell me," Slick's good paw reached out and touched my cheek softly.

"Every night, before I go to bed, I check the ewes to see if any of them look like they might lamb soon," I began. "And I get up every night at 3:00 to look again. It's so cold out there for a brand new lamb coming into the world. I want to make sure the mother licks it dry and it gets some warm milk into its stomach, or it'll die."

Slick nodded with his eyes.

"Last night, Maynard and I looked at the ewes, and we decided none of them looked close to lambing. I decided not to get up at 3:00. After all, it was Christmas — why not sleep through the night this one time?"

"I understand."

"When I went out to chore this morning, a ewe was standing by herself, away from the herd. She was crying. I went to look closer, and beside her . . . beside her in the snow were

two nice big lambs . . . frozen, dead."

"Oh no!"

"Yes. I wanted to scream, hit something, hit myself! It was my fault! Why didn't I get up during the night? I was so mad! It was a beautiful Christmas morning, but all I could see was two frozen little white lambs, and all I heard was the mother crying for her babies."

"But Carol, maybe they were born dead. Or maybe they were born after 3:00 and you wouldn't have been there anyway."

"Maybe. But I don't know that. I only know that I failed. I was a bad shepherd, Slick."

"And how many times have you been a good shepherd?"

"What do you mean? I don't know."

"I know. I see you out there all the time, for hours in the cold. I see you rescuing baby lambs. I see you bringing them in and back to life when they seem as good as dead. I've seen it."

"Well that's what you do when you have sheep."

"Exactly. That's what you do. Now you have one time when

some lambs died. If you want to blame yourself, go ahead. But then you'd better learn to forgive yourself too. Forgive yourself, take a lesson from it if you want to, and go on."

I didn't know what to say. I felt like crying some more, to say goodbye to the guilt and pain and wash it away. So I did, and Slick closed his eyes.

Later, when my crying was over, Slick opened his eyes. "How did you get so wise?" I asked him softly.

"Some things you just know from being there," he said. "Goodnight."

"But what do you mean?"

Slick had his eyes closed again, and this time I had a feeling he wasn't going to open them to answer my question. And I got to wondering how he'd learned about forgiveness. I got to wondering what happened to his right front leg — why it was folded back like that. That leg was useless to him, but he'd never told me why. I had a feeling he never would.

"Goodnight, Slickfester Dude," I whispered.

Corby and Emma

It was 10 p.m. on a winter February evening, and I was soaking under a pile of bubbles in the bathtub. Slick showed up, looked at me, looked at the bubbles, and then back at me.

"You don't usually take a bath in the evening," he stated.

He was right, of course. I usually run in the morning and take a bath after that. But tonight I had a good reason to be in the hot water.

"This hasn't been a usual kind of evening," I answered Slick. "I need to warm up. I got very cold and wet tonight."

"Oh?" said Slickfester Dude, climbing to the edge of the tub. "What happened?"

"Well, you know I have two lambs, Corby and Emma, that I'm feeding with a bottle. I decided to take them to youth group tonight to be a part of the lesson."

"I bet the kids loved that. What was the lesson about?"

"First, I told them about Corby. She was a quad — her mom had four lambs, and Corby was the last one. By the time she had Corby, she figured she'd had enough, and she didn't accept the last little girl lamb. So Corby became my bottle baby."

"Yes, I've heard her crying for her bottle," Slick commented.

"I told the kids that Corby and I are good friends, and that Corby loves and trusts me because I'm the one who has always given her food. But Emma is a different story. Emma was a triplet, and her mother loved and accepted her. When Emma was a few weeks old, it was obvious she wasn't getting enough milk from her mom. So I decided I would have to give her some milk from a bottle too. But Emma didn't know me like Corby did. I had to catch her to give her the bottle."

Slick began to laugh. "I think I've seen that. At least I've seen you sneaking up on a lamb, lunging at it, and sometimes you get it and sometimes you don't. I think I've even seen you fall down a time or two," he chuckled some more.

"Not funny, Slickfester Dude," I said, turning on some more hot water.

"Oh yes it was," he said. "But go on."

"Obviously, Emma doesn't trust me. But just two days ago, we finally stopped this chasing game. She realized that if she stood still and came up to drink the bottle, it was a lot easier on both of us. But that's the only time she gets close to me — when she can see the bottle."

"So you had Corby and Emma running around in the youth group?"

"Yep. And I said that our relationship with God is a lot like that. Sometimes we are Corbys and sometimes we are Emmas. Sometimes we feel really close, and sometimes we just go to God when we want something. I asked the kids to think about whether they were a Corby or Emma right now in their life, and then we went around the

room and talked about that. There were a lot of Emmas in our group
that evening."

"Okay, it sounds like an interesting lesson, but I still don't understand how you got cold and wet."

"I took Corby and Emma to church in the trunk of my car. When Maynard and I took them back out to the car and put them in the trunk, Emma jumped out and started running."

"Oh no."

"Oh yes. Now Slick, here's the scene. Tabor Church is in the country, surrounded by farms and fields and pastures. It's dark. The church yard light illuminates a little past the church yard, into the fields around it. Emma ran across the yard, through the ditch, and into the field, with this 40-plus year old woman running after her screaming 'Emma! Emma!' You get the picture?"

"I do. A fast, scared lamb and a desperate middle-aged woman."

"Hey, not middle-aged!"

"Face it, Carol, you are. Now go on!"

"Emma ran away from the church, into the dark, through the field, and I ran after her, panting her name. Every once in awhile she'd stop and look at me. She knew something about me was familiar, but she was scared, and she didn't trust me. I'd get almost close enough to grab her, but not quite. And she'd turn and run again."

"Coyote food," said Slickfester Dude.

"Exactly. I knew if I didn't catch her, she'd be lost forever. Yes, probably a nice meal for a hungry coyote. So I kept running and calling. Through a farmyard. Into a pasture. Through tall grass, where I could just barely see her ahead of me. I saw that she was heading for a creek."

"Cold and wet."

"Yep. I figured the creek would slow her down, and I'd grab her before she got to the other side. She hit the water, I hit the water, she jumped up on the bank and was running before I could reach for her. Now I was wet. And Emma was running toward a barbed wire fence that bordered the pasture. If she got through that. . ."

"Coyote food," Slickfester Dude repeated solemnly.

"I was so out of breath, so desperate, so scared of losing her. She ran into the fence and I just fell on top of her, holding her, panting. And about that time, the electric fence that was in front of the barbed wire fence zapped me."

"OUCH!" Slick cried, and his eyes got real big.

"It got me once, then again! I wasn't letting go of that lamb for anything. Finally I managed to roll away from the hot wire and I just lay there, holding Emma, breathing hard."

"But you got her!"

"Yep I did. Maynard picked us up, we came home, I dried Emma off the best I could, and she's back with the sheep herd. And I'm taking a hot bath with lots of bubbles."

"I understand," Slick sighed. "That was quite an experience. Do the youth group kids know what happened?"

"Nope. We took the lambs out to the car at the end of the meeting, and we just never made it back. We'll tell them next week. And we'll tell them the meaning behind the story."

"Which is?"

"God never gives up on you, even if you are an Emma."

"It's a good thing to know," said Slick. "A very good thing to know. Thank you for telling me that story. I'm going to bed now."

"I'll be there soon, Slickfester Dude."

Di Gets Stuck

"Di told me what happened today," Slick said one evening. "It sounded like an awful experience."

"I know what it was like for me, but I'd like to hear what she told you."

"She said you and the dogs went running, and the labs chased up a rabbit. Di followed him into a culvert, and she got about half-way into the culvert before she realized that mud had washed into it. The farther into it she went, the smaller it got. Before she knew it, Di was stuck. She couldn't go any farther, and she couldn't back out."

I could almost see a shudder sweep through Slick's body.

"You know, Carol, I watch my whiskers. If they don't clear the sides, I don't go in. The thought of being stuck like that gives me the willies."

"Tell me about it."

"Di was terrified. She hoped and prayed you would miss her, and would hear her barking. Which of course you did."

"Yes, I could hear her barking but I couldn't see her from the end of the culvert. It was dark and she was way in there."

"Di said she couldn't see anything behind her, but she heard you talking to her. She heard you crawling in there after her. She was so happy to hear you, but she was really scared too, because she figured if she got stuck, you might get stuck too. And then who would find you two? How many hours would it be until they missed you, and how would they know where to look? That's what Di was thinking."

"Well she wasn't the only one thinking that. I actually tied a dog leash to my ankle in case someone would have to pull me out, but that wouldn't help until they found me. There's not much traffic on that country road, you know. That's why it's so great for running. Anyway, the further I went in there, the tighter it got. I was pulling myself on my elbows, and it got so tight I realized I couldn't reach forward to Di even if I got close enough. That's when I almost panicked."

This time a visible tremor shook Slick. "I'm panicking now just hearing you talk about it," he said.

"I started backing out. Slowly. Inch by inch. Telling myself to be cool. Push backwards. It's okay. Push backwards. It's okay."

"Hurry up!" Slick said, and I had to laugh. I was glad it wasn't him stuck in the culvert instead of Di.

"Finally I got out and took a deep breath of fresh Kansas air. But Di was still in there."

"She told me she knew you got out, and then she didn't hear anything for a long long time. She knew you wouldn't forget her, but she felt terrible. It was dark and muddy in there. She was stuck. And she felt bad for being such a problem for you. All because of a stupid rabbit who was small enough to get out the other end."

"I didn't know what to do, but I decided to call a

friend of ours who worked with the county road crew. He said he'd talk to the other guys and see what they could do. A little later, they drove on the yard here at the farm, and we all went to the part of the road a mile away where Di was stuck in the culvert."

"Di said she heard the truck and road maintainer, and she heard your voice. She cried with relief, she said."

"The guys began to dig up the road to get to the culvert. That must have been scary for Di."

"Yes, it was. But she said she trusted that you wouldn't let anything happen to her. She just kept telling herself it would be okay, and you would take care of her. She could hear the equipment scraping the dirt off of the top of the culvert. It hurt her ears to hear that so close — scrape, scrape, scrape. Then they were moving the dirt away from the sides. She wanted to believe they couldn't hurt her, but it sure didn't feel like that with that big equipment so close. And then, all of a sudden, the culvert was being lifted out of the ground, and she slid out the end. You came rushing over to see if she was okay," Slick said.

"She seemed okay to me. Did she tell you she was all right?"

"She said she was fine. Embarrassed, and her pride was hurt. And she said she'll know better than to get into a tight spot like that again. Not for a rabbit, not for anything."

"I'm glad to hear that. I'm not sure the road crew would be thrilled to come dig out the culvert again."

"Did they charge you a lot of money?"

"Nope. They smiled and said 'Your county taxes at work.' Made my day, it did."

"So what do you think the lesson is?" Slick asked.

"Pay your taxes?" I asked.

"No, silly. Don't get

yourself in tight spots. And if you do, and you're fortunate enough to have a friend bail you out, learn your lesson and don't do it again."

"Oh," I said. "I'll remember that."

"Watch your whiskers," added Slickfester Dude, and he began to take a bath.

"I will. Goodnight, Slick."

BJ and Her Babies

"Let's talk about BJ," Slick said one evening as he started to take a bath on the bed.

BJ is a beautiful silver-gray Persian cat — the mother of many litters of kittens on our farm.

I wondered why Slick wanted to talk about her, but he usually had a good reason.

"Okay, let's talk about BJ," I agreed.

"Have you noticed how she never has much to say . . . until she has kittens? Then she talks all the time."

Yes, I had noticed that.

"When they're first born, all she can talk about is how cute they are," Slick continued. "And of course we all have to agree."

"Well, they usually are quite cute."

"Not right at the beginning," Slick argued. "Anyway, about the time they get cute, she's talking about how they're eating her out of house and home, and she's begging you for more food."

He was right again. BJ begged for food a lot when she was nursing her babies.

"And then there's the in and out thing," Slick continued. "She wants to go outside because she doesn't know what to do with the babies anymore, and then she wants to come in because she can't be away from them."

"Slick, all cats do the in and out thing. You know that."

"Well she's especially bad when she has kittens."

"Okay, go on."

"You know what she does next. She starts inviting them into the kitchen. It's not good enough anymore for them to be in the utility room," Slick said. "Why, I've heard her actually say, 'Come here kids, you won't believe the fun stuff to play with in this part of the house.'"

"Yep, you're right."

"And the next thing you know, they're running all over the house and BJ is having a terrible time keeping track of them."

"She's a good mother, that's for sure."

Slick stared at me after I said that, then he asked, "Why? Why would you say that?"

"Well, she's proud of them when they're born. She feeds them well, and she's concerned about what they're doing. And she encourages them to go out and explore new areas, even if she can't be watching them all of the time."

"She should be a good mother. She's had plenty of practice."

"True. You know what I think?" I asked.

"What?" said Slick.

"I think BJ could have been a beauty queen with a great

career, but it was more important to her to raise many wonderful children."

"And we get to listen to her talk about it."

"It's a small price to pay to be able to give away such well-adjusted kittens," I said.

"As long as you keep giving them away, I can live with it," said Slick. "Goodnight."

"Goodnight."

Somewhere downstairs we heard a chorus of meows that sounded a lot like kitty-goodnights.

Pete Goes For A Run and A Ride

"I saw something funny today," Slick said, chuckling his way across the bed one summer evening.

"And what was that?" I asked, putting the book down that I'd been reading.

"A white pickup drove in the yard, and for the life of me it looked like Pete was driving it."

I laughed. Pete, our quite overweight chocolate labrador, driving a pickup? I could picture it now. Actually, I'd seen it myself. And I knew the story behind it.

"Yes, I know, I saw it too," I agreed.

"What was going on? Whose pickup was that?"

"Our neighbor Erna's. Actually, she was in there too, and she really was doing the driving."

"It looked to me like Pete was the one behind the wheel."

"Well, Slick, here's what happened. I went running today, with all of the labs, as usual. And as usual, Pete couldn't keep up. Mo and Flicka and I came home, but Pete didn't."

"Where was he?"

"Who knows? I think he followed the other dogs into some fields, and was just a lot slower in getting out. By the time he did, they were long gone."

"Were you worried about him?"

"Not really. At least not right away. This has happened before. And he's always made it home before. Well, a few times I've had to rescue him."

"Today was a very hot day for a fat dog to be jogging," Slick observed.

"You're right. That's why, when I saw our nice neighbor Erna hauling wheat to town in her pickup, I asked her to keep an eye out for Pete. She said she sure would. Erna's one of those people who'll do anything for you. She said she'd try to find Pete for me, but I figured he'd probably make it home on his own."

"But he didn't."

"Nope. Erna showed up on the yard with him in her truck. She told me what happened. She said she was driving down the road when what should she see ahead of her but big Pete, slowly trotting down the middle of the road, panting hard. She stopped the truck and said 'Hey Pete, jump in and I'll give you a ride home.' But Pete is so fat he can't get himself up into a truck. So Erna went around and helped lift him into the passenger side of the truck. Then she got in on her side and began to drive to our farm."

"I'm sure Pete was very grateful," Slick commented.

"Pete was so thankful that he kept scooting closer and closer to Erna to tell her how thankful he was. She'd say, 'It's okay, Pete.' But he'd just sit closer and closer until he almost pushed her out the door."

"And that's why it looked like Pete was driving the truck."

"Yep. And that's why Erna probably looked and smelled like a hot dog had been slobbering on her. But she didn't mind at all. She was just happy to help."

"She's a good neighbor," Slickfester Dude said.

"That's for sure," I agreed.

"Who knows what could have happened to Pete, trying to find his way home in the hot sun?"

"Who knows? I'm glad he's home. I wouldn't have been able to sleep very well if he was out there somewhere tonight."

"Thank God for good neighbors," said Slick, yawning. "Goodnight."

"Goodnight, Dude."

Reebok's Job

One evening Slick came scurrying across the bed and I knew he was eager to tell me something. He didn't even sit down before he started.

"I saw Reebok telling Selena secrets," he stated, standing in front of me, his tail twitching with excitement.

Reebok is a tall white llama who lives with the sheep herd. Selena is a small black and brown Nubian goat who also hangs out with the sheep.

"What makes you think Reebok was telling Selena secrets?" I asked.

"Well, when we cats touch noses, we're talking to each other. Sometimes we're telling each other the rules of the house or something new that we just found out. That's what Reebok and Selena were doing."

"Touching noses?"

"Yep."

"That's a long stretch for Reebok, way down to little Selena. But then, it's part of his job, I suppose."

"What do you mean?" Now Slick was the one asking questions.

"I mean it's Reebok's job to keep track of the sheep and goats, let them know what's going on, and watch out for them if it looks like anything bad is going to happen."

Slick settled down in front of my face and said, "Is that why he was crying the other day? I'd never heard him do that before. I'd heard him hum for his grain — I guess that's kinda like singing for his supper, isn't it?" Slick chuckled at his little joke. "Anyway," he continued, "What happened?"

"What happened was that one of the goats — not Selena, a different one — got into the lamb feeder and I didn't want her in there eating the lambs' grain. So I snuck up behind her and grabbed her by the back leg. She started screaming like she was being mortally wounded."

"Oh yes, I can hear her now. The end of the world."

"Well the minute she started hollering, Reebok came running over there, and he was extremely worried. He was doing a high-pitched noise that sounded like a cry saying 'Oh no! Something terrible's happening! Oh no!' He was quite upset about whatever was making the goat scream."

"Why was he so concerned? The goat didn't belong in there. Why did he even care about a goat that was misbehaving?"

"It's his job. He's with our sheep and goats to watch out for them. He loves them. They're his family."

"And what happened when you let the goat down and she stopped screaming?"

"Reebok went over to make sure she was okay, and then he checked out the rest of the herd, and he hummed a lot. Finally he was satisfied that everything was okay."

"Very interesting," said Slickfester Dude.

"Personally, I find it very comforting."

"You mean that he's taking care of your sheep for you?"

"Yes, that too. But I find it comforting because if Reebok takes his job of caring for his family so seriously, imagine how serious God is about taking care of us people. It's God's job, you know."

"Wow," said Slickfester Dude. "It's God's job to watch out for you? That is a very comforting thing to know."

"For sure," I said.

"I like that," said Slick. "Sleep good, Carol."

"I will. You too, Slickfester Dude."

Zora's Tale

"Tjej heard from another one of her daughters today," Slick said one evening as he climbed up onto the bed and reached for my hand.

"That woman gets more mail than I do," I said.

"Maybe it's because she has more children," Slick commented. "This time it was Zora, and she didn't send just a letter. There was a videotape too!"

"Really! Did Tjej show it to you?"

"Yep. And it confirmed what I've said all along. Those Siamese are strange."

"Does Zora carry a sock too?"

"Nope. It's crazier than that," Slick said, and started laughing. "You really should see the tape."

"Okay, do I have to go downstairs and watch it right now?"

"No," Slick giggled. "I'll tell you, and you can watch it tomorrow.

See, Zora gets on a padded folding chair. You know, the kind with the short back."

"Yes."

"She climbs up on the back of the chair and hangs over the top and then guess what she does?"

"Just tell me, Slick. I don't want to guess. I'm kind of tired tonight."

"Okay, okay. She hangs over the back edge and goes after her tail, which is of course dangling behind her and visible from where she's hanging. She tries and tries to get it and every time she stretches farther to get it into her mouth, it just gets farther out of reach. Isn't that just crazy?"

"I agree. That's crazy."

"When she finally does manage to catch it, she's terribly embarrassed because she realizes it's her own tail!"

Slick and I laughed together, and then he said, "Silly Siamese, working so hard to get something that's hers all along."

"Well, if she's a silly Siamese, I can't say us people are much better a lot of the time."

"I don't see you chasing your own tail," Slick said.

"No. But, for example, sometimes I get all worked up trying to earn God's love and forgiveness. Too often we humans try so hard to do the right things so we can deserve God's love, when it's really there all along."

"Like Zora's tail."

"Yep. We don't have to chase God's love, just accept it. It's already ours."

"You really should watch the video," Slick said, and then yawned real big.

"I will. Goodnight, Slick."

"Goodnight."

(Zora's Tale by Charity Bucher, Hillsboro, KS.)

The Willies

"It's your turn to tell a story," Slick announced one evening, and there really was no arguing with him. He'd just sit there and stare at me until I did. So I did.

"This is a story about the Willies," I began.

"You mean the heebie jeebies?" Slick asked.

"No, the Willies. Now listen, or I won't tell it."

"Okay, okay."

"A number of years ago, during lambing time, I noticed a small white object way out in the pasture, all by itself," I began. "I went out to see what it was, and sure enough it was a baby lamb. Its mom had gone off and left it."

"Why?"

"Who knows? Although I soon found out one possible reason. The lamb couldn't stand — its legs didn't seem to work. And it had a dent in its forehead. A big flat spot where it had either been kicked or stepped on, or maybe it was born that way. I don't know."

"How awful."

"It was. I brought the little girl lamb home, and began to feed it with a bottle. Surprisingly, even though it couldn't stand and had a strange dent on its head, she learned how to nurse right away. She obviously wanted to live."

"Good girl."

"I named her Willie, after Willie Shoemaker the jockey. He had an accident that put him in a wheelchair, but it didn't daunt his spirit. I saw the same determination in my little lamb that he must have."

"Oh, I get it now. Willie."

"Yep. For several days, Willie ate and responded to my care, but she couldn't stand. Then, very slowly, her legs began to cooperate. By the time she was a week old she was standing pretty good, and although she still had the strange mark on her head, it didn't seem to affect her. She grew like any other lamb, and became a part of our herd of sheep. But she did keep one problem that may have come from being a bottle baby — she had a persistent cough. Sometimes, it seems like bottle babies drink the milk so fast they get a chronic cough — something in their lungs that never goes away. Willie had that kind of cough. But a year later, as an adult ewe, she gave birth to a little baby girl of her own, and I was so happy."

"It made it all worthwhile, didn't it?" Slick said.

"That's right. But one morning, Willie was coughing a lot, and breathing hard, and she wasn't getting up. Her three-week-old baby just stood beside her, wondering why her mother wouldn't stand up. It didn't look good. Later, I checked on them, and Willie had died. Her little girl was beside her, taking a drink now and then from her dead mother. I was very sad, but I was glad that at least Willie had left a little girl behind to carry on her legacy. And so she became my bottle lamb, and I named her Willie, of course."

"Of course."

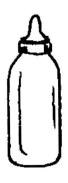

"That Willie grew up to be a ewe in our herd, and you know what happened this spring?"

"I could guess but you go ahead and tell me."

"She had a little baby girl."

"That you named Willie?"

"Nope. Only bottle babies get names. And Willie is raising her daughter just fine all by herself."

"So you had two Willies."

"Two Willies and hopefully generations to come from the second Willie and her daughter."

"And all because the first Willie really wanted to live, even though she had some tough stuff to face in the beginning."

"Exactly. You're getting good at finding meanings in stories, Slick."

"You told a good story."

"Thank you, Dude."

"We make a good team, don't we," Slick said, giving me his paw.

"We do indeed," I agreed.

Nikki and the Guinea

"Those boys are quite something," Slick said one evening after we'd had my relatives over for supper. "They can wear a cat out."

Slick was talking about my young nephews, Travis and Kent.

"But one time they actually sat still long enough to tell me a story," Slick continued.

"Really? What was it?"

"Well, they have a dog, Nikki. She's a big white dog, and she seems to like guineas. You know, those noisy fowl things we have here too."

"Yes, I know. And dogs have been known to enjoy guineas. I guess they're too much like chickens."

"Probably, because every once in awhile, a sad little pile of feathers would show up in the yard, and there'd be one less guinea."

"Did they try tying Nikki up?"

"Yes, and that seemed to be working. They were down to two guineas — a husband and wife. And the wife was sitting on a nest of eggs. Then one day she was gone."

"Nikki?"

"Nikki said she didn't do it. In fact, she insisted that Mr. Guinea got real brave and attacked her if she even came close to the nest. Nope, she didn't kill that guinea, she said. Some outside intruder did it."

"So then what happened? As Paul Harvey would say, what's the rest of the story?"

"The one lonely Mr. Guinea started hanging around with Nikki.

Wherever Nikki was, there he was. If Nikki was in her dog house, the guinea could be counted on to be nearby. They actually seemed to be friends."

"Friends?"

"Go figure. I don't understand it either. And when the people and Nikki went for a walk, the guinea went too. Until he got tired and started to complain. You know how guineas can complain."

I nodded. It is very hard to ignore a complaining guinea.

"He finally flew back to the yard and waited for everybody to return. He raised a ruckus, of course, until they came back."

"That is so strange. What do you suppose happened to make the guinea and the dog become friends?"

"Travis and Kent said they figured the guinea had been reading the Bible."

"The Bible?"

"You know, that part about loving your enemies and doing good to those who hurt you."

"Oh, that part," I said.

"Does the Bible really say that?"

"Yep. In fact, it was Jesus himself who said it."

"Hmm...mm...mm." Slick closed his eyes, and I wondered if he'd fallen asleep. But after a little while he opened them again and looked at me. "That's a pretty good lesson, isn't it?"

"It sure is, Slickfester Dude."

"Well then, I'm glad the boys came over tonight and told it to me. Even if the rest of the time they wore me out."

"Get a good night's sleep, Slick."

"I will," he yawned. "Goodnight."

"Goodnight, Dude."

Arthur

"There's a lamb out there wearing a green collar and a tag," Slick said from the end of the bed one spring evening. He three-legged his way toward me and sat down. "Is he special or what?"

"Yes, he's very special," I answered. "His name is Arthur. He was born the day we met an 89-year-old attorney named Arthur who had personally invited us to a speaking engagement. I sometimes have a tough time coming up with new names, so it's always neat when a lamb is born the same day we meet somebody special. That way I can name the new lamb after that person."

"'I'm glad his name wasn't Willie 'cause we have too many Willies already," Slick said with a silly grin. "But that still doesn't explain how come he has a collar and a tag, when none of the others do."

"None of the other bottle lambs get letters and presents from an attorney — or from anyone, for that matter."

"You mean Arthur gets letters from Arthur?"

"Yep. And the lamb writes the man back too."

Slick stared at me with his "I don't believe this story" look. "So let me guess," he said. "Arthur the man sent Arthur the lamb the collar and tag."

"You got it."

"Well that explains it. Having an attorney friend will get you special treatment every time."

"No, Slick, in this case it's just having an 89-year-old friend who still gets a big kick out of life — including having a lamb named after him."

"So what happens to Arthur the lamb when he grows up? I don't see a lot of adult male sheep around here."

"You're right, Slickfester Dude. We give the boy lambs to God. That will have to include Arthur."

"You give the boy lambs to God?"

"Yep, we have a deal here that all of the boy lambs born on our farm go to God."

"Who made that deal? You or God?"

"Well I think we all agreed on it."

"What does God want with your boy lambs?"

"Actually, it's a little bit more complicated. We sell the lambs and the money we get goes to people and places that do God's work. And there's a lot of that to be done."

"But that means you're giving up half of your lambs."

"Approximately, yes. It's always kinda fun to see when a lamb is born — if it's going to be ours or God's."

"You don't ever think God tweaks the numbers a bit, do you?" Slick's eyes were laughing.

I laughed too. "Yeah, this year it almost looked like it. But that's okay. God's been mighty good to us, so I guess we'll take our chances."

"And you're actually going to give up Arthur the special lamb?"

"That one will be harder. In fact, he's already missed the first couple of trips to town. But he'll go one of these days. It's part of the deal."

"And you're sure this deal is as good for you as it is for God?"

"Believe me, Slickfester Dude, it is. It's called stewardship. I know that's a big word to throw at you, but it just means giving back to God because God has given to us."

"Okay," said Slick. "I believe you. And you're sure you don't pray for girl lambs?"

"No, Slick," I chuckled. "Are you ready to go to sleep now?"

"Yep," said Slickfester Dude.

"Me too."

The Return of Reuben

Slick had been telling me stories for a long time, and one of the things that happened over the months and years was that Reuben the pug became blind. Pug dogs seem to have problems with their eyes, and Reuben had been in accidents that caused him to lose sight in both of his.

One evening when Slick came to bed, I had a story for him. "Slick, remember, a long time ago, you told me the story about where Reuben goes?"

"Sure I remember."

"I have one to tell you. It's kind of about where he goes, but different."

"I'm listening."

"As you know, Reuben is blind. He gets around in the yard okay, but we try to watch that he doesn't go too far, because he'd get lost."

"Yep, I've had to bring him back a few times."

"Yesterday, I couldn't find Reuben. I called and called. I looked in all of his favorite sleeping places. He wasn't there. I looked where I thought he might like to sleep, but he wasn't anywhere. When Maynard came home, I told him. He looked. We went out on the road to see if he'd been hit there. Nothing."

"And no pigs in the mud for him to be visiting?"

"No. No pigs in the mud. We got very worried. A small fat blind dog out in the countryside overnight — bad things could happen to him. We finally had to quit looking and go to bed, hoping he'd show up in the morning."

"That was this morning?"

"Yes. But no Reuben. I spent a lot of the day, looking for him and calling. When Maynard came home from work, he went driving and looking. While driving, he talked to God. He said he would like to find Reuben, alive or dead. He just wanted to know that he wasn't suffering someplace without food or water, unable to find his way home. It would be an awful way for a little dog to die. That's what hurt Maynard the most — the not knowing. So he prayed that we'd find Reuben soon, one way or the other."

"Did he find him?"

"No. He came home. And when he drove in, Reuben was sitting in the middle of the yard."

"You're kidding."

"Nope."

"So where was he?"

"God only knows."

Slick looked at me with those big gold eyes — a look I'd gotten so used to over the years. "You probably mean that literally, don't you. That part about God knowing."

"Well Slick, it's like this. Reuben was gone. We couldn't find him. We prayed. Reuben came back. I don't know how or why. But I choose to believe. I choose to believe God cares about us, and about Reuben."

"It's a good thing to believe," said Slick. "Goodnight."

"Goodnight, Slickfester Dude."

Slickfester Dude's

Photo Album

The following photo album shows you a few of my people and animal friends at Willow Spring Downs. Maynard and Carol invite exchange students to live with them every school year, so that's why a lot of my people friends are from Germany and Sweden.

Marten Olsson came to Kansas from Sweden and made friends with our raccoon, Dundee.

I'm keeping my German friend, Martin Altstaedten, company while he takes a cat nap.

Gabi Karolji, from Sweden, with our thoroughbred mare named Tell Me A Story (she had that name when we got her. Pretty neat for our family, huh?) Carol and Gabi named Story's colt Flying Fiction — Fly for short.

Story, the thoroughbred mare, had a mule named Running Rhyme. As you can see, Rhyme didn't run very much, and she didn't obey Maynard either.

A scene outside my window one winter day: Cole Traumuller from Germany, and Mo enjoying the snow.

He's such a begger, that Spike. Here he's got Cole feeding him ice cream.

77

Silke came from Germany to visit Martin. She and Mo Dog got to be good friends.

Fresca sent Tjes this picture of Grandma Goossen with Pepsi and Paytuh. Tjes doesn't have a photo album, so I put it in mine.

It's a toss-up who was the sweetest — Swedish Madde Svensson or one of Flicka's chocolate puppies.

Carol left on a business trip. Her best goat-friend died. So Maynard bought her Selena for her birthday. Julia Brandstatter, from Germany, really fell in love with Selena. She's okay — for a goat.

Lisa Karlsson and Spud. They got along great! But when Lisa's dad from Sweden rode Spud, Mr. Karlsson ended up walking home and he still doesn't remember what happened!

These are two of my favorite friends — Reebok the llama and Selena the Nubian goat. I'm glad they like each other too.

Cattis Frostner from Sweden got to feed the lambs when Carol was gone on a business trip. She did a good job!

We see Carol doing a lot of this during lambing time.

Tyey, that
strange
Siamese.

Tyey gave Lloyd
the sock for his
nap time.

Happy Jack hangs around and looks nice so people will take pictures of him. It works.

Elsie (L.C.) is named for Lisa Christine because she was born the day Lisa's parents came to visit from Sweden. Elsie's really sweet. So are Lisa & her parents.

Pete is tolerating a chocolate puppy while Flicka just watches. (See how fat Pete is?)

Mr. Peacock shows off a lot. He'll even do it for the goats.

Stupid Goat (yes, that's her name) is always reaching for green stuff beyond where she's supposed to be. She's just a stupid goat but she has cute kids.

I don't know their names. They're sweet, and they're for sale.

This
is
me.

These are my
people —
Maynard
and Carol

Other Books from WillowSpring Downs

Jonas Series

The Jonas Series was the brainchild of Maynard Knepp, a popular speaker on the Amish culture who grew up in an Amish family in central Kansas. Knepp and his wife Carol Duerksen, a freelance writer, collaborated to produce their first book, *Runaway Buggy*, released in October, 1995. The resounding success of that book encouraged them to continue, and the series grew to four books within 18 months. The books portray the Amish as real people who face many of the same decisions, joys and sorrows as everyone else, as well as those that are unique to their culture and tradition. Written in an easy-to-read style that appeals to a wide range of ages and diverse reader base — from elementary age children to folks in their 90s, from dairy farmers to PhDs — fans of the Jonas Series are calling it captivating, intriguing, can't-put-it-down reading.

Runaway Buggy

This book sweeps the reader out of reality into the world of an Amish youth trying to find his way "home." Not only does *Runaway Buggy* pull back a curtain to more clearly see a group of people, but it intimately reveals the heart of one of their sons struggling to become a young man all his own.

Hitched

With *Hitched*, the second installment in the Jonas Series, the reader struggles with Jonas as he searches for the meaning of Christianity and tradition, and feels his bewilderment as he recognizes that just as there are Christians who are not Amish there are Amish who are not Christians.

PREACHER

Book three in the Jonas Series finds Jonas Bontrager the owner of a racehorse named Preacher, and facing dilemmas that only his faith can explain, and only his faith can help him endure.

BECCA

The fourth book in the Jonas Series invites readers to see the world through the eyes of Jonas Bontrager's 16-year-old daughter Becca, as she asks the same questions her father did, but in her own fresh and surprising ways.

SKYE SERIES

A spin-off of the much-loved Jonas Series, the Skye Series follows Jonas Bontrager's daughter Becca as she marries and becomes the mother of twin daughters, Angela and Skye. While Angela rests on an inner security of who she is and what life is about, Skye's journey takes her to very different places and situations. Through it all, she holds tightly to one small red piece of security — a bandanna her Amish grandfather gave her as a child.

TWINS

In the first book of the Skye Series, Becca and her husband Ken become the parents of twin daughters through very unusual circumstance — circumstances that weave their lives together even as they are pulled apart by their separate destinies.

ORDER FORM

Jonas Series: *($9.95 each* **OR** *2 or more, any title mix, $10 each, we pay shipping.)*

_____ copy/copies of *Runaway Buggy*

_____ copy/copies of *Hitched*

_____ copy/copies of *Preacher*

_____ copy/copies of *Becca*

Skye Series:

_____ copy/copies of *Twins* @ $9.95 each (to be released Oct 1, 1997)

Other:

_____ copy/copies of *Slickfester Dude Tells Bedtime Stories* @ $9.95 each

Name _____

Address _____

City _____ State _____

Zip _____ Phone # _____

____ Book(s) at $9.95 = Total $ _____

Add $3 postage/handling if only one copy _____

SPECIAL PRICE = Buy 2 or more, pay $10 each and we'll pay the shipping.

Total enclosed $ _____

Make checks payable to WillowSpring Downs and mail, along with this order form, to the following address:

**WillowSpring Downs
Route 2, Box 31
Hillsboro, KS 67063-9600**

For more information or to be added to our mailing list, call or fax us on our toll-free number
888-551-0973